Check out these other exciting
▼ STECK-VAUGHN
Science Fiction Titles!

How far would you go to break into
the movies? Get the answer in
BEHIND THE SCREAMS

Here today . . . gone tomorrow!
Find out more in
WARP WORLD 3030

It's alive. It's growing. It's *hungry.* See why in
BZZZZ

Earth is in for a big jolt. Check out why in
SHORT CIRCUIT

There's a whole lot of shakin' going on!
Read all about it in
SUPER STAR

What *are* those robots talking about?
Find out in
THE LOST LANGUAGE

All that glitters isn't good! See why in
CHARMERS

History can really get to you! Learn more in
BLAST FROM THE PAST

This fan is out of this world!
Find out why in
ALIEN OBSESSION

ISBN 0-8114-9328-8

7 8 9 06 05 04

Produced by Mega-Books of New York, Inc.
Design and Art Direction by Michaelis/Carpelis Design Assoc.

Cover illustration: Tom Roberts

COSMIC EXCHANGE

by Ann Richards

interior illustrations by
Keith Neely

STECK-VAUGHN
ELEMENTARY · SECONDARY · ADULT · LIBRARY

A Harcourt Company

www.steck-vaughn.com

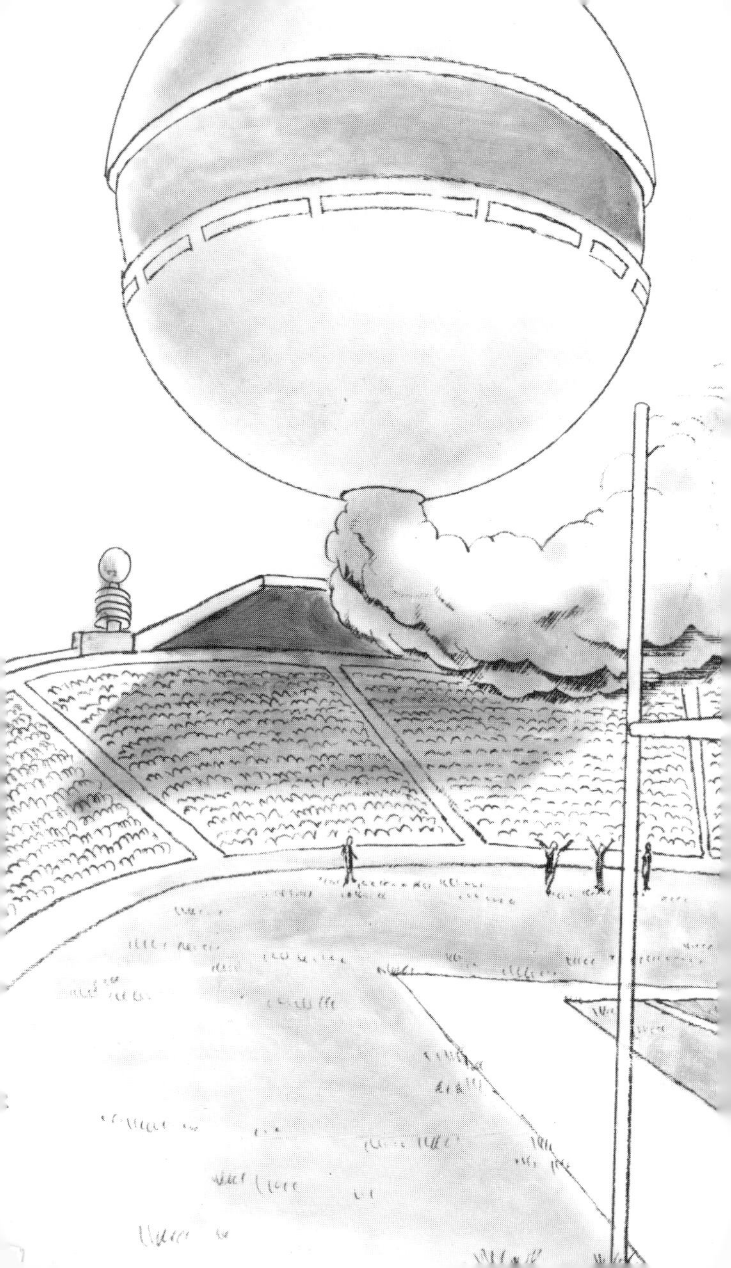

CHAPTER
1

Greg Walsh tightened his grip around Eliza Cooke's shoulders. They watched the enormous spaceship begin its descent onto Sanger High's grassy football field.

It was the first time Greg or Eliza had seen a real spaceship up close. Space travel was becoming common in the 21st century. But it was usually politicians who journeyed to other planets in the Milky Way galaxy—not high school students.

Now everyone at Sanger High School was soon to be an instant celebrity. Sanger was the first high school to participate in a student exchange program between two planets.

Classes had been canceled that morning. Now the students were gathered in the bleachers at the football stadium for the biggest event ever to happen at their school.

A burst of steam exploded from the underside of the spaceship.

Eliza held her breath. She couldn't believe that in a few minutes this spaceship from Planet Pax would land at her own high school. Vron Athmar, the exchange student from Pax, would spend an entire month attending Sanger classes and living with Eliza and her family. The Cookes had been chosen by the school committee to be Vron's host.

Eliza glanced over at Darryl Pollock, Greg's best friend. He would soon board the spaceship to travel to Pax as the exchange student from Earth.

Darryl was busy clowning around. Eliza guessed he was trying to hide his nervousness. "I wonder if Vron will be

nervous, too?" she thought. "What if he doesn't speak English? How will we communicate?"

If Vron was anything like Greg or Darryl, she doubted she'd have much to talk about with the Paxan anyway.

Conversation was not one of the boys' strong points.

Greg's idea of a date was to go to a movie, then meet up with friends afterwards for pizza. He and Eliza almost never had an evening alone together, just talking and hanging out.

But Greg was the most handsome boy at Sanger and a great athlete. Eliza loved sports, too. She was a starter on the girls' basketball and volleyball teams. She was also an excellent swimmer, and taught swimming during the summer. Eliza liked playing basketball with Greg. She just got bored talking about it so much.

Still, she had hoped there would be more to their relationship than practicing their foul shots every Saturday afternoon.

Eliza wondered what Vron would look like. She knew a little about Paxans from a course she had taken last semester on intergalactic studies. But no one on Earth had ever seen someone from Pax in person. And there were no pictures or photographs of the Paxans at all.

The Paxans didn't have cameras, television or videotapes.

Eliza's intergalactic studies teacher had explained that the Paxans' hearing and sense of smell were more highly evolved than Earthlings'. They didn't rely on visual stimulation for entertainment. Instead, the Paxans combined special fragrances with music to produce symphonies for the ears and nose.

The spaceship landed gently on the field and immediately a ramp extended from the belly of the ship.

Music blared from the ship's exterior as a small human-like form walked down the ramp.

"It's like a music video," said Greg. He, Eliza and Darryl were standing next to Sanger's principal as part of the

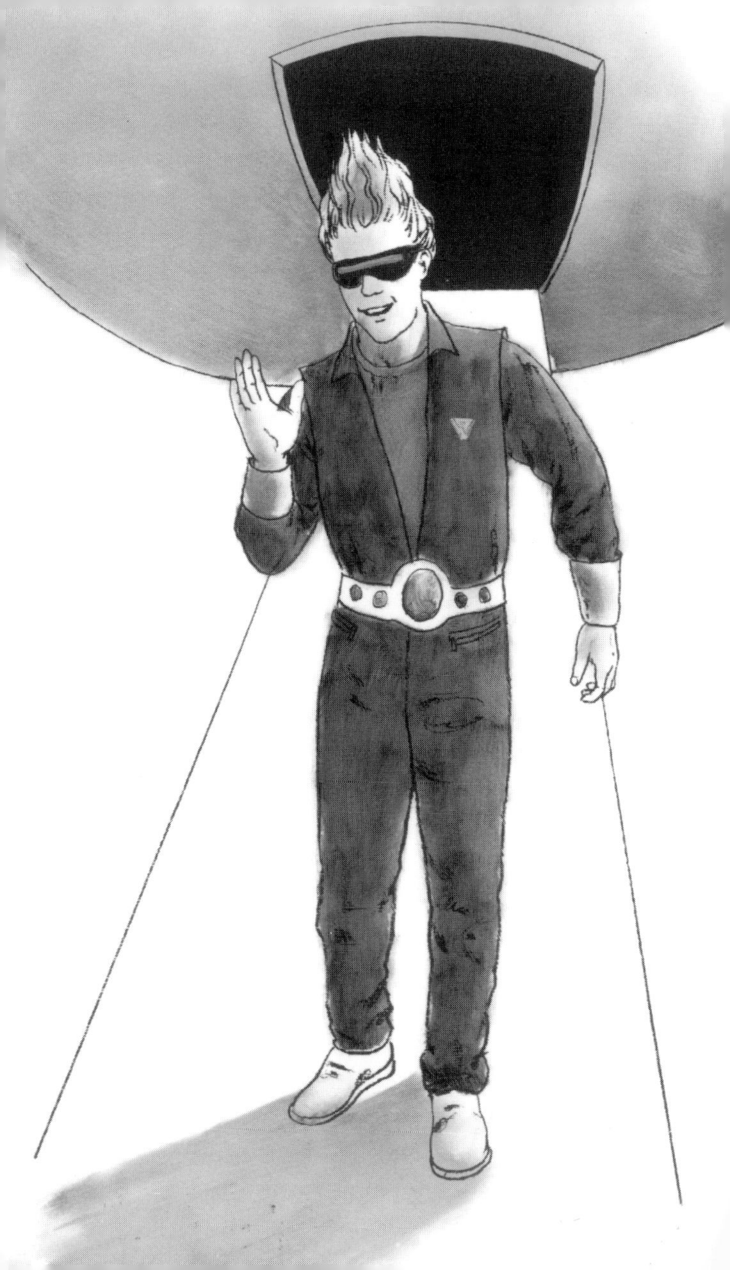

official welcoming committee.

Hundreds of pairs of human eyes were focused on the Paxan as he approached the welcoming committee.

The first thing that stood out about Vron was his hair. It was bright purple and rose from the top of his head in stiff curls. But other than that, Vron looked like the average Sanger High student.

He wasn't as tall or broad-shouldered as Greg or Darryl, but Vron looked very athletic. There was something cat-like about him. Maybe it was the black jumpsuit he wore, or the wraparound sunglasses that gleamed with reflected sunlight.

"Cool sunglasses," said Darryl. "I wonder if I can get a pair like that when I get to Pax."

"I love his hair," said Eliza. "It's wild!"

Greg glanced at Eliza. He didn't like the way his girlfriend's eyes sparkled as she looked at the Paxan. "He looks like the toy troll my kid sister got for her birthday," said Greg.

The principal shook Vron's hand. Then Greg presented Vron with a Sanger High varsity jacket. It was much too big for Vron's slender frame. But Vron accepted the jacket with a smile and thanked Greg. Then he turned to face the students in the bleachers.

"Thank you, all," he said in a friendly voice. "It is an honor for me to be here and I hope that my visit will be the first of many future interplanetary student exchanges."

Loud applause and cheering shook the bleachers.

Greg shrugged. "That guy seems kind of nerdy, don't you think?" he said to Darryl.

"I don't know," Darryl answered. "At least his speech was short. I hadn't thought about giving a speech when I get to Pax. Maybe I'll just repeat what Vron said." Darryl jotted Vron's words down in his notebook.

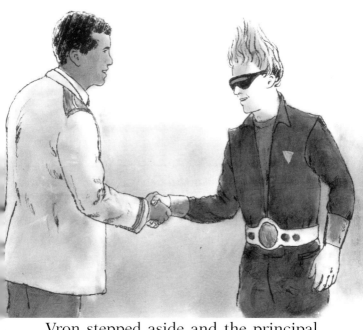

Vron stepped aside and the principal addressed the crowd. "Thank you, Vron," he began. "I know I speak for everyone here at Sanger in extending to you our warmest welcome."

The principal's voice droned on. Eliza noticed that Vron was the only one who seemed to be paying attention.

"And so," the principal concluded, "it is now time to bid Darryl Pollock goodbye and good luck." The principal put his arm around Darryl's shoulders. "Farewell, Darryl!"

The students jumped from their seats and gave Darryl a standing ovation as he walked up the ramp. At the top, just before he entered the spaceship, Darryl paused and waved to the crowd. Then

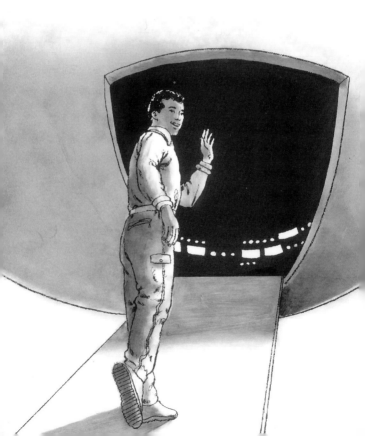

he turned and disappeared into the ship. The ramp retracted, and the spaceship started steaming.

A moment later, the spaceship zoomed into the sky and disappeared in the clouds.

"All right, students," the principal said. "Back to classes!"

Groans filled the bleachers as the students began to move toward the school building.

But Eliza wasn't complaining. As part of her host duties, she was to show Vron to all of his classes. She was looking forward to getting to know this stranger from another planet.

CHAPTER
2

Vron's first week at Sanger was the best week of school Eliza had in a long time. Vron was interested in every detail of high school life on Earth. Eliza found herself looking at everyday things as if she, too, were seeing them for the first time.

Vron wanted to blend in with the other teenagers at Sanger High. His black jumpsuit and wild hair had attracted too much attention. He couldn't walk down the street without stopping traffic. So Eliza took him shopping. He bought clothes and shoes like everyone else had. But he kept his sunglasses, which Eliza assured him

would start a fashion craze on Earth.

Vron also wanted to do the same things kids on Earth did—especially dance. So Eliza threw a dance party in Vron's honor that Friday night. She invited the entire senior class to her house.

After greeting most of her guests, Eliza put on The Plutoniums' newest laser disc and asked Vron to dance.

Vron's body moved as if he were part

of the music. Everyone at the party stopped to watch Vron and Eliza shake, twist and spin to the music. When the song ended, there was loud applause.

"Come on," suggested Eliza. "Let's get something to drink." She led Vron to a long table covered with snacks and fruit juices. She poured herself a glassful of orange juice. "What would you like to drink?" Eliza asked Vron.

"Paxans don't drink liquids," Vron said. "But I love Earth food." He helped himself to a handful of pretzels.

Eliza noticed Greg standing over by the window. He waved at her to join him. She shook her head 'no' and mouthed, 'later.'

Greg rolled his eyes and looked away. Eliza wished Greg wasn't so jealous. But she had to admit being with Vron was more fun than she ever had on any of her dates with Greg.

The party was a huge success. Eliza knew that Sanger students were as curious about Vron as he was about Earthlings. One reason she had given this party was so her friends could get a chance to talk to Vron. And there was definitely a crowd at the snack table now. Everyone was eager to chat

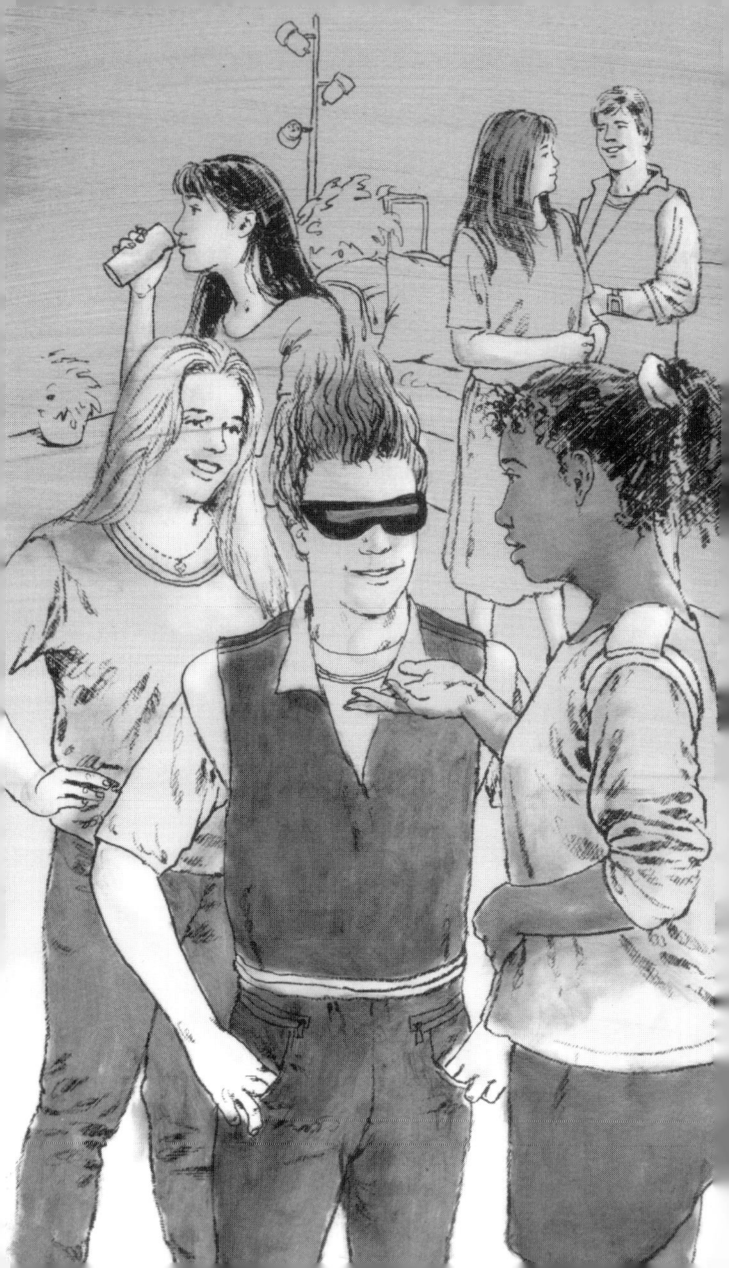

with the Paxan. Vron was eager to talk.

"Do you have a girlfriend?" One of Eliza's friends, asked Vron.

Eliza blushed. She was embarrassed that anybody would ask such a personal question.

But Vron didn't seem to mind. "On Pax, we do not date as you do here on Earth. We must focus on our education and family responsibilities until we have finished school."

Vron answered a few more questions about life on Pax. Then he suddenly excused himself and took Eliza's arm as he steered her outside onto the porch.

"What's wrong?" asked Eliza. "Were they bothering you?"

"No," Vron said. "I just wanted a moment alone with you."

To her surprise, Eliza felt her heart skip a beat.

Vron reached into his pocket and pulled out a small box. "I have a gift for you." He opened the box and removed a crystal pendant which hung from a delicate silver chain. "Thank you for being such a good friend," he said.

The crystal sparkled with different colors as it caught the light from inside.

"It's beautiful," Eliza said. "It's like wearing a rainbow."

"On Pax, we cannot see the colors you describe," Vron said softly. "For us, the crystal's beauty is in the delicate music it makes. It sounds like a million tiny wind chimes swaying in a morning breeze."

Vron stood behind Eliza to clasp the necklace around her neck. As he leaned forward, his cheek brushed lightly against Eliza's.

"Hey, what's going on?" Greg shouted as he rushed out onto the porch. "Get your hands off my girlfriend!"

Eliza gritted her teeth to keep from saying something she might later regret.

"Hello, Greg," said Vron. He finished fastening the necklace. "I was just about

to tell Eliza the story of this pendant. As you may know, our eyesight is not nearly so evolved as yours. We sometimes cannot distinguish people by sight, even among our own family members. On Pax, everyone wears one of these crystals. It gives off a unique sound. That way, we always know who is nearby."

"I don't hear anything," said Greg.

"I don't either," said Eliza.

"Some day you will," Vron said to

Eliza. "You just have to *really* listen."

Greg shifted his weight from one foot to the other awkwardly. He felt a little foolish, realizing Vron and Eliza hadn't been kissing as he thought. Vron was just giving her some dumb Paxan rock.

"Well, I gotta go," Greg said. Then he briskly wrapped his arm around Eliza. "I'll pick you up tomorrow night at the usual time."

"I can't go out tomorrow night," Eliza said quickly. "I'm spending the evening at home with my family and Vron."

"Oh," said Greg. He let his arm fall from her shoulder. "Well, okay. Bye." Greg tried to hide his disappointment as he walked away.

But he couldn't shake his thoughts free of Vron and Eliza.

Since Vron had arrived, Eliza had spent every moment with him. Now she was going to spend Saturday night with him, too!

"This extraterrestrial dweeb isn't going to steal my girlfriend," Greg said to himself as he walked to his car. "I'll make sure of that!"

Sunday morning, Greg jogged over to the basketball court at school. His buddies Dean Rayson and Kyle Lee were already there shooting hoops.

"Hey, Greg," shouted Dean. "How's it going?"

"Okay," said Greg. He grabbed the

ball and threw it in for an easy lay up.

"So what's with Vron and Eliza?" asked Kyle as he tried to block Greg's next shot. "They've been like glue since he got here."

"Nothing," said Greg, faking to the left, then pivoting around to the right past Kyle.

"That's not what Amy told me at breakfast this morning," said Dean, grabbing the ball and taking an outside shot. It bounced off the rim. Kyle rushed in for the rebound.

Greg grabbed the ball from Kyle, stopping the game. "What exactly did Amy say?" he demanded. Dean was Amy's brother. Amy was Eliza's friend.

"Hey, cool down. It's probably nothing," said Dean.

"Out with it," insisted Greg.

"Amy said that Eliza thought Vron was cute." Dean grabbed the ball out of Greg's hands and scored a three-pointer.

"Well, I think this extraterrestrial

Romeo needs a lesson," said Greg. His voice was laced with venom. "And I don't mean in the classroom."

CHAPTER

3

When Vron and Eliza got to school Monday morning, Greg was already waiting for them on the steps.

"Hi, Greg," said Vron.

"Hey, Vron. I'm glad I caught you. Some of the guys are playing basketball after school today. I thought you might like to give it a try."

"Basketball?" Vron looked at Eliza for an explanation.

"It's a popular sport. The object is to throw a ball through a hoop," Eliza answered. She stared at Greg.

"Sure," Vron said to Greg. "Thanks, I'd like to play basketball."

"Good. Meet us on the court behind

the school after your last class." Greg gave Eliza's arm a squeeze and ran up the steps into the building.

"That was nice of Greg to ask me to play," said Vron.

But Eliza wasn't so sure. She knew Greg was mad at her about missing their Saturday night date. And she remembered his ridiculous behavior at the party.

Some girls liked it when their boyfriends were jealous. But not Eliza. She wished Greg would just go back to being the same sweet guy she'd first been attracted to. She even missed his stupid jokes. But since Vron had arrived, Greg had definitely lost his sense of humor.

Eliza forced these thoughts from her mind as she and Vron headed in for first period class.

When Vron got to the basketball court that afternoon, Greg was already warming up with Dean and Kyle.

Eliza had explained to Vron the rules of the game in more detail that day at lunch. She had a meeting with her own varsity team after school, so she wouldn't be able to watch.

Vron put his books down on the ground and jogged over to the guys clustered around the basket.

"Hi, Greg," Vron said.

"Hey, buddy" said Greg. He

introduced Vron to Dean and Kyle.

Winking at his friends, Greg threw the ball hard at Vron's stomach. Vron didn't see it coming. He doubled over as the ball knocked the wind out of him.

"You and I will play Dean and Kyle," said Greg as Vron recovered.

A few kids on their way home stopped to watch the action. Greg's plan was working. He knew a lot of students

walked by the basketball court on their way home. He was counting on them hanging around to see the Paxan be humiliated at basketball.

Every time Vron got the ball, Dean and Kyle double-teamed him till he made a turnover. They showed no mercy. And they both fouled Vron over and over again. But there was no referee to blow the whistle.

"It's not fair," said Amy, watching the game. "My brother and Kyle are ganging up on him."

"Vron's so much shorter than the others," said another girl.

"Yeah, but he's got more style than all three of those jocks put together," said a third girl.

Greg overheard the remarks. His plan was backfiring! Instead of thinking Vron was a nerd for not being good at sports, everyone was siding with him!

In anger, Greg threw a pass hard toward Vron's head. Even Dean and

Kyle would have dodged it. But Vron jumped into the air, caught the ball and slam dunked it right into the basket!

The crowd went wild, cheering loudly for Vron.

It was as if Vron's feet had sprouted wings. Suddenly he was making jump shots from the outside and rebounding balls before Dean or Kyle could even touch them.

It only took a few more minutes for Vron to win the game with a perfect half-court shot that swished right through the net.

Greg was speechless. He couldn't believe it. After a weak start, Vron had played like a top professional.

"I thought you said the dude couldn't play!" said Dean.

"I said he couldn't *see*," Greg countered. "I didn't know he could jump like Michael Jordan from twentieth-century days."

Eliza rushed up with Amy and congratulated Vron. "I'm glad I got out of my meeting in time to see the last minutes of the game!" Eliza said. "You were great!"

"Fantastic!" agreed Amy.

"It wasn't so difficult once I knew the height of the basket," Vron replied.

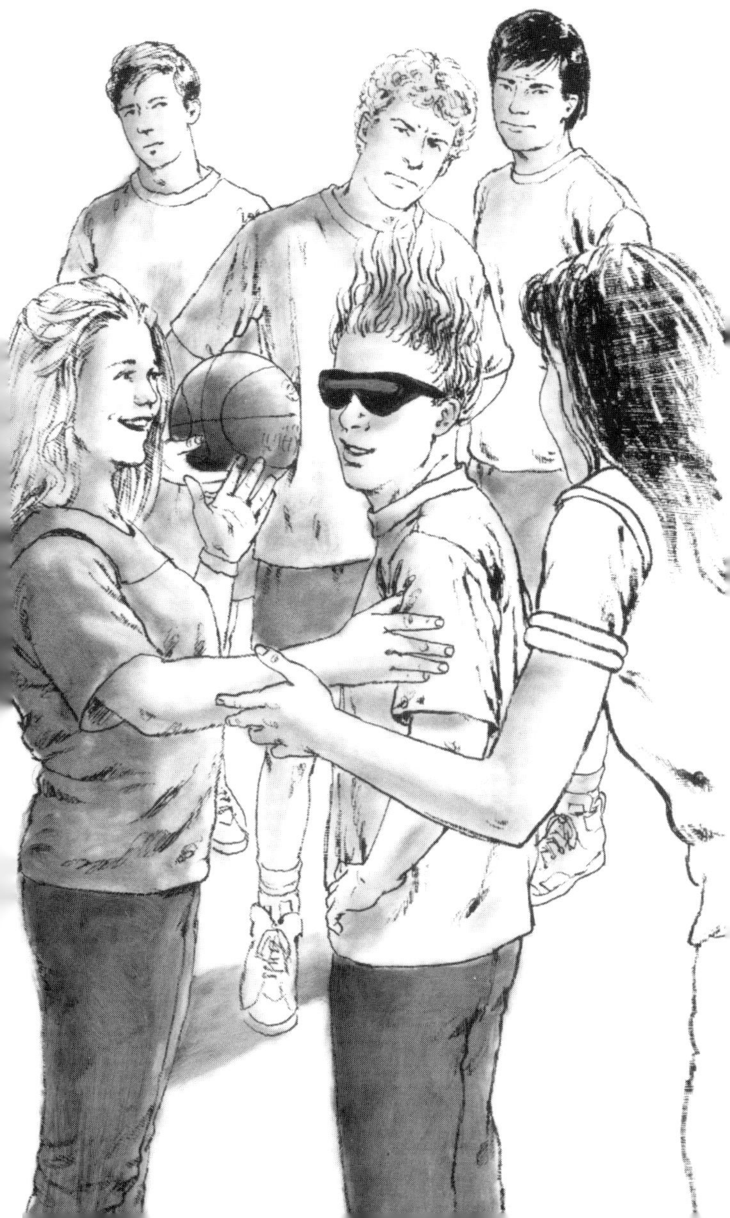

"After I heard the ball hit the rim a few times, I knew where the basket was. I calculated the distance to the net from every point on the court. Then it was just a question of the angle I needed to get the ball through the net without bouncing it off the rim. A very interesting game!"

"You mean you used math to make those shots?" Amy asked.

"Of course," answered Vron. "Isn't that how everyone plays?"

"No," explained Eliza. "They aim the ball and hope to throw it just hard enough to get it through the basket."

"You mean they guess?"

"Well, sort of. The best players have a feel for it," Eliza said.

"That seems impractical to me," said Vron. He looked puzzled.

Eliza laughed. "It probably is!"

Greg and his buddies walked over to Eliza, Vron and Amy.

"Good game," said Dean. He shook

hands with Vron. "Where'd you learn to jump like that?"

"On Pax, the gravitational pull is much stronger than it is here on Earth. I find I can jump much higher here than on Pax."

Kyle gave Vron a friendly slap on the shoulder. "Too bad you can't stick around all year. We sure could use you during the playoffs."

Dean, Amy and Kyle were still talking about Vron's last shot as they walked off the court.

"Well, I guess we'd better go or we'll be late for dinner," said Eliza. She waited for Greg to congratulate his teammate. But Greg just scowled.

"Bye," Eliza` called to Greg as she turned to go. She was getting tired of Greg's jealousy. She missed the old Greg. Maybe she should make more time for him. But Vron was only here for another three weeks. There was a lot she still had to show him about life on Earth. "Greg and I will have plenty of time to see each other after Vron leaves," Eliza reasoned.

Greg didn't see it that way. He was furious. His plan to show up Vron in front of Eliza and the rest of the students had failed miserably.

And now he was losing Eliza, too.

If only Vron would just hurry up and go back to Pax.

CHAPTER
4

Greg dug around the bottom of his closet. He searched for the old music synthesizer he had gotten for his thirteenth birthday a few years back.

Finally, he found it beneath a pile of dirty clothes and old sports equipment.

The music synthesizer was about the size of his computer keyboard. It had a built-in mini-compact disc recorder so he could play his music back.

Greg had a new idea for how to get even with Vron.

He set the synthesizer to its highest pitch and started pounding on the keyboard.

The next day at school, Eliza and

Vron were a few minutes early to their first period History class. Vron's four-week visit was almost half over. It seemed to Eliza as if he had just arrived.

The history class was studying 20th century fictional heroes that week. The teacher brought in old books, videotapes, and comic books. Some of them were a hundred years old!

Just before the bell, Greg strode into class with Dean and Kyle. They sat in their usual spots in the back of the class. Eliza watched them pass. Before Vron came, she and Greg had always sat together.

"Today, we're going to talk about Superman," said the teacher. He projected a large image of the super hero on the big screen in front of the classroom. "Nice costume!" joked Amy.

The class discussed the differences between Clark Kent, Superman's alter ego who posed as a regular Earthling, and Superman, the hero from Planet Krypton.

"Hey, Vron's kind of like Superman!" exclaimed one of the boys in class.

Just then Vron let out a bloodcurdling scream and jumped out of his seat. His hands flew to his ears, and he ran from the classroom.

The class was stunned. They stared at the door, wondering what had happened to the Paxan.

Greg's giggles broke the silence. "I guess Superman had to use the men's room!" He burst into laughter. Dean and Kyle, who had been in on Greg's prank, started laughing, too.

Eliza glared at Greg. Whatever had just happened, it was obvious that Greg had something to do with it. She rushed out after Vron.

"What happened?" she asked when she caught up to Vron in the hallway. "Are you all right?"

Vron was massaging the side of his head behind his ears. "It was the strangest thing, Eliza," Vron said. "There was suddenly this incredibly loud, screeching sound. It was awful! I thought my ears would burst!"

Vron was angry. Very angry! It was the first time Eliza had seen him that way.

"What do you think caused it?" she asked in a worried voice.

"I don't know. But whatever it was, it

came from inside the classroom. I'm sure of that," Vron said.

Eliza thought of Greg and his friends laughing in the back of the room. She was determined to find out what was going on.

After her last class, Eliza waited for Greg at his locker.

"Hey, gorgeous," said Greg. He leaned

in to give Eliza a kiss, but she jerked her head away.

"What did you do to Vron?" she demanded. "You could have broken his eardrums!"

"I don't know what you're talking about," Greg lied.

44

"Yes, you do," insisted Eliza. "Ever since Vron arrived, you've been jealous of him. I'm not blind. I saw how rough you were playing basketball the other day. I tried to convince myself that's just how guys play. But now you've gone too far!"

"Look, Eliza," said Greg. He tried to take her hand, but she pulled it away and folded her arms across her chest. "I'm sorry. You're right," Greg continued. "I was jealous of you and Vron. Who wouldn't be if his girlfriend was spending every waking moment with another guy?"

"I'm not dating Vron," Eliza said defensively. "He's a guest here and I'm just doing my job as host."

"Well, I think you're going above and beyond the call of duty," Greg said angrily. "I think you like the guy and you'd rather spend time with him than with me." Greg slammed his locker shut in frustration.

"Maybe I would," said Eliza. "Especially since you're acting like a total jerk!" With that, Eliza turned and quickly walked away.

CHAPTER
5

During Vron's third week at school, the senior class gathered in the auditorium. They were going to participate in an interactive television transmission from Pax to Earth.

Darryl had brought an earth-linked satellite camera with him to Pax. Now he would emcee this historic event. Not only would it be the first time images were transmitted from Pax, it was also the first time young Paxans and human teenagers would communicate directly.

Vron was seated at the front of the auditorium next to the big screen monitor. He would act as translator.

Eliza was sitting with Amy near the

front of the auditorium. Greg came in and sat in the empty seat on the other side of Eliza. Eliza didn't even acknowledge him. She hadn't spoken to Greg since their fight.

Greg figured that a shot of romance was what he and Eliza needed. He had made reservations at Casa Italiana for that Saturday night. Now all he had to do was ask Eliza out. It would be a challenge, since he had already phoned her several times and she hadn't taken his calls.

"If only I could get her alone," he thought. "Then I could apologize."

But Eliza was never alone! Either she was with Vron, or Amy, or surrounded by classmates asking about her Paxan house guest. It was a big break to find that empty seat next to Eliza. Greg knew he had to try to get through to her. It was now or never.

Greg leaned in towards Eliza and whispered, "Let's go out Saturday night.

Just the two of us. I want to take you to
a new restaurant."

Eliza didn't answer.

"Please, Eliza," Greg whispered. "I
know I was acting like a jerk. I want to
make it up to you."

Eliza sighed. Maybe she should give
him a chance. "All right," said Eliza. "I'll
go out with you Saturday night."

"Great!" Greg breathed a sigh of
relief. That wasn't as hard as he thought

it would be. He sat back with a smile.

The big screen started to flicker. The students stopped chatting in anticipation of what was to come. Suddenly Darryl's picture, bigger than life, filled the screen.

"It's Darryl!" shouted a boy sitting in the back.

"Dar-ryl!" another yelled.

Soon the whole room was chanting, "Dar-ryl! Dar-ryl!"

The students were clapping their hands and stomping their feet. The whole room was shaking.

"All right, students! Calm down!" demanded the principal.

The room quieted down. Darryl began to speak. "Fellow Sanger High students," he began. "Before I open the discussion to questions from my Paxan hosts, I want to share with you what I've discovered these past two weeks on Planet Pax."

"He seems different," Eliza said to

Greg. "A little more, I don't know, relaxed."

Greg shrugged. He had never paid that much attention to how Darryl behaved—except on the basketball court.

"The first thing I noticed about Pax is how brightly colored everything is," said Darryl. He gestured behind him as the camera panned the landscape. The sky shone with pink hues and the ground was dark blue.

"It's beautiful!" whispered Eliza. "I'd love to go there."

"Yeah, you probably just want to spend more time with Vron," Greg thought. He frowned.

"Paxans pride themselves on their self-control and patience," Darryl continued. He spoke for a few more

minutes about Pax and its customs. Then he introduced Krex, who had the first question from Pax.

Krex looked like Vron, but his hair was yellow instead of purple.

Vron translated. "Krex asked, 'What is chocolate?' "

The Sanger students laughed. Several raised their hands to try to answer Krex's question.

The question-and-answer session went on for about half an hour. Most of the questions focused on food, clothes and music.

Vron translated the last question from Pax. "What are your favorite activities?"

"Basketball!" shouted Dean.

"Tennis!" yelled Amy.

"Swimming!" called Eliza.

Vron translated their answers.

"What's swimming?" asked a Paxan.

"You jump into the water and move your arms and legs to propel yourself forward," Eliza explained.

The Paxans were silent.

"Did I say something wrong?" Eliza asked Vron.

"No, Eliza," Vron said. "It's just that on Pax we are forbidden to touch water."

"Why? What would happen if you did?" asked Eliza.

None of the Paxans answered. None of them had ever touched water to find out.

The picture on the screen started to flicker as the camera zoomed in on Darryl. "That's it for now!" he said. The screen went blank.

"That's strange, don't you think?" Eliza said to Amy.

"What is?" Amy asked.

"About water. I knew Paxans didn't drink water. But I didn't realize they couldn't even touch it."

"I wonder what would happen if Vron got caught out in the rain," said Amy. "Maybe he would melt like the Wicked

Witch in *The Wizard of Oz*." Amy and
Eliza had read all the Oz books last
semester in a class on 20th-century
fantasy and science fiction.

"I think Vron is more like Superman
than the Wicked Witch," said Eliza.
"He's got special hearing like
Superman."

"Yeah, and he sure can fly!" added
Amy, remembering the basketball game.

"All he needs is a cape to go with his
jumpsuit," said Eliza. She and Amy

55

burst into laughter. They didn't notice that Greg had been listening.

Students started to rise and file out of the auditorium.

"See you later, Greg," Eliza said as she left for her next class.

"Maybe Vron's like Superman," Greg thought to himself. "But even Superman has a weakness—a big weakness."

CHAPTER
6

On Saturday afternoon, Eliza took Vron out for a rocket-skating lesson. Rocket skating was the newest fad to hit Sanger High.

Vron and Eliza strapped on the solar-powered skates. Eliza taught Vron the basics of stopping and turning in a nearby parking lot.

Vron caught on immediately. After a few minutes practice he was as good as Eliza.

Soon, they were skating easily up the sidewalk. Earlier, Eliza had given Vron a map of the area to memorize so he wouldn't have to rely on his poor eyesight to guide him.

"So, you like skating?" asked Eliza.

"Oh, yes," Vron answered. "It makes me feel like a regular Earthling teenager."

"Well, you certainly skate like one!" said Eliza, impressed.

"But why do the other students still call me Superman?" Vron asked.

"They know you can hear better than they can. And they probably want to know if you have other super powers," Eliza replied.

Suddenly Vron started to skate ahead of Eliza. She tried to catch up. "Slow down, Vron!" she called out to him. But Vron sped away. Eliza had never seen anyone skate so fast!

Vron turned a corner and was completely out of sight.

"Vron!" Eliza called. "Wait!" She sped after him. When she rounded the corner, she saw a truck barreling down the hill. It was out of control! And it was heading right for two young children on robo-bikes! The children froze.

Eliza's hands flew up to cover her eyes. She waited for the sounds of a crash and screams.

But there was only silence. Eliza took

her hands away from her face and opened her eyes.

The children were laughing with relief. The robo-bikes were untouched. And Vron was standing by the stopped truck, talking to the driver.

Eliza skated over to them.

"What happened?" she asked the truck driver. "I thought you were going to hit those kids!"

"So did I," said the truck driver. "My brakes failed going down that hill. Then I saw this purple-haired boy skating right along next to me. I must have been going over eighty miles an hour! The next thing I know, he's under my truck and I jerk to a stop. If it wasn't for your friend here—I don't want to think about what might have happened!"

"I heard the truck picking up speed," Vron explained to Eliza. "From the map you gave me, I knew it should be braking for the hill. I could hear that the truck wasn't going to stop on its own, so I stopped it."

"How?" Eliza asked Vron. "It was going so fast!"

"I slid under the truck and fixed the brakes," explained Vron.

"I don't know how you did it, son," said the driver. "But I'm glad you did. I guess I'd better call for a tow truck." The driver walked off in search of a pay phone.

Some parents who had seen Vron stop the truck came over to thank him. A few minutes later a television news van pulled onto the scene to interview the Paxan.

Vron was a hero!

"How about some pizza?" Vron suggested to Eliza after the crew left. Since he had arrived on Earth, Vron had discovered all kinds of junk food. He loved French fries and greasy burgers. But pizza with extra cheese was his favorite.

"Sounds good to me," said Eliza.

When they arrived at Eliza's house a couple hours later, Eliza saw Greg's car in the driveway. "Oh, no!" she cried. "I forgot all about my date with Greg!"

Greg was watching television with Eliza's dad when Eliza and Vron came in. He was all dressed up. A bunch of flowers lay limply on the coffee table.

"I'm really sorry, Greg," Eliza began. "Vron saved this truck from . . ."

"Vron!" Greg shouted. "It's always Vron! I'm sick and tired of hearing about Vron!"

Before Eliza could explain, Greg angrily stormed out of the house, flowers and all.

CHAPTER
7

Vron's last week at Sanger High passed quickly. He had made friends with some of the students and was participating in lots of activities, so he didn't need Eliza so much.

Eliza found herself with more free time on her hands. Without Vron to entertain, she began to think about Greg again. But even though she missed him, Eliza felt that Greg owed her an apology for his jealous behavior.

And Eliza was torn. She was dreading the day when the Paxan spaceship would arrive with Darryl to take Vron back home.

Meanwhile Greg couldn't wait till the

day Vron would leave Earth forever. Greg had his own personal going-away gift for the Paxan. With the help of his friends, Greg began to put his plan into action.

The night before Vron was to leave, Eliza ordered three large pizzas with extra cheese and invited Amy and a few other friends over to watch videos. She had invited Greg and his buddies, but Greg told Eliza he had something else to do. Kyle and Dean couldn't make it either. Eliza wondered if Greg was dating another girl.

Amy was the first to arrive at Eliza's house. "Hi, Eliza." She looked around the room. "Where's Greg?"

Eliza was surprised to feel her eyes tearing. "He couldn't make it," she said. "He had other plans."

"What's wrong, Eliza?" asked Vron. "You sound so sad."

"Oh, nothing," Eliza lied. She didn't want to bore Vron with her romantic problems. And she was afraid she would start to cry.

"She and Greg broke up," Amy confided to Vron.

"Amy!" Eliza wished her friend would keep her mouth shut.

"Is that true, Eliza?" asked Vron.

But Eliza didn't answer. She hadn't admitted her fight with Greg could mean they had probably broken up forever. She had told herself that when

Vron left, everything would go back the way it had been.

"Yes, it's true," Amy answered for her friend. Vron look worried.

But Eliza barely heard Amy's words. She held back her tears as she answered the doorbell. More guests were arriving.

While Eliza, Amy, Vron and others were solemnly eating pizza and talking

about teenage life on Earth, Greg, Kyle and Dean were sneaking around behind the school.

"I think I found it," said Dean. He shone his flashlight on a metal box in the ground. He popped the box open with a screwdriver. Kyle and Greg leaned over him.

"The timer is set for seven in the morning," Dean explained. "That's

when the sprinklers usually go off. But when I push this button the time changes. See?"

"Great!" said Greg. He would finally get his revenge. "After this farewell present, that Paxan won't ever want to come back to Earth!"

The next day, exactly four weeks after his arrival, Vron made his good-bye speech to the students of Sanger High. Many of the students still suspected that the Paxan had special powers, like Superman, and that he was hiding them. They watched him eagerly, hoping he would perform one last exciting feat.

"Thank you all very much," Vron began. "This experience has taught me so much about Earth and its wonderful people. But I have also learned a lot about myself. And this new knowledge will help me . . ."

Suddenly water started squirting up from the ground all around the podium

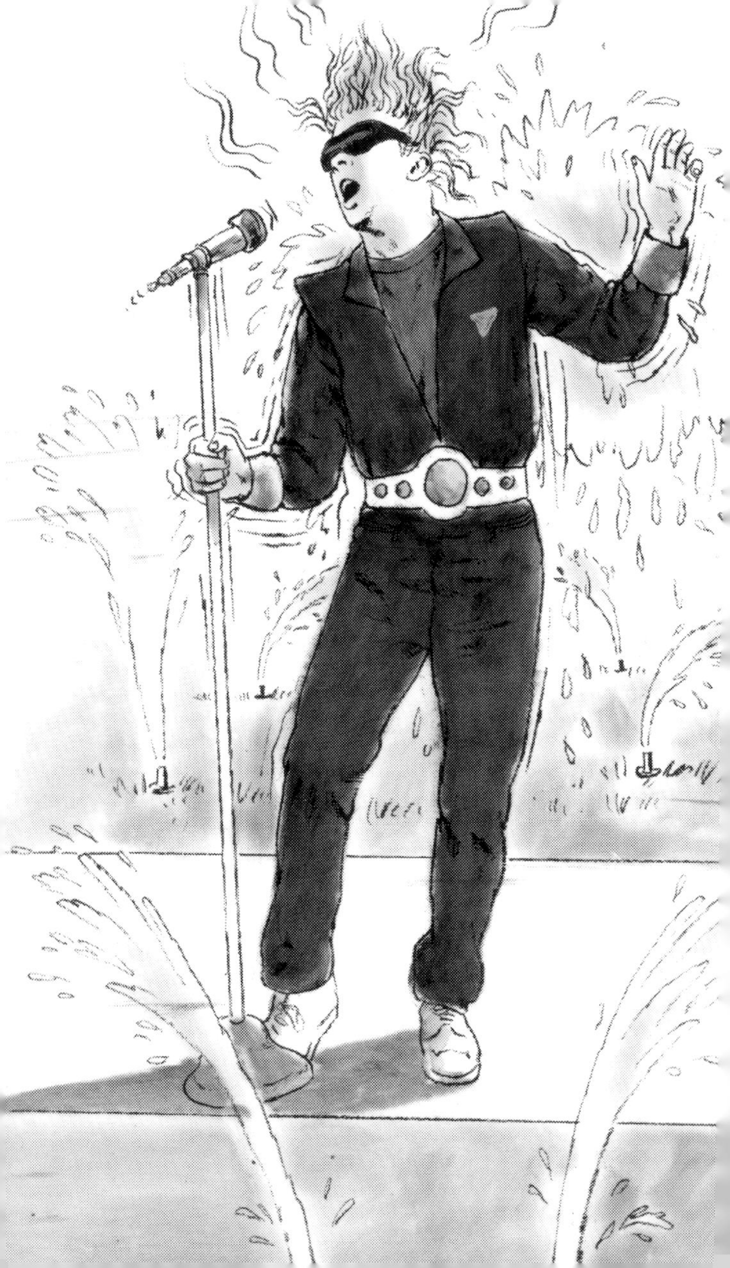

where Vron was speaking. As the drops of water hit Vron's body, he began to tremble and shake.

His arms flew out from his sides and his knees buckled. Vron's purple hair fell limply to his shoulders.

The students watched in horror as Vron's skin started to sizzle. The sound was horrible.

Then the Paxan collapsed. He lay motionless on the ground.

CHAPTER
8

"Vron!" Eliza cried. She rushed over to Vron's lifeless body. "Someone cut off the sprinklers!" she yelled.

"Is he alive?" Amy cried, following close behind Eliza.

"The water killed him!" another student shouted.

Greg ran over to Eliza. His face was white with fear. "I didn't mean to kill him!" he said. "Please, Eliza, you've got to believe me. I'm so sorry!"

The last drops of water hissed against Vron's skin. Slowly he opened his eyes. "What happened?" the Paxan whispered to Eliza.

"The sprinkler system must be

broken," said Eliza. "It turned on while you were speaking." She wasn't ready to tell Vron that Greg had planned this disastrous stunt. She was afraid of what Vron might do. Eliza hadn't forgotten how mad he had gotten after

Greg's nasty synthesizer prank.

"It was no accident," Vron said angrily. He weakly stood himself up. The students cheered in relief.

"I would like to end my visit to Earth with a demonstration of some special Paxan powers," Vron announced. "I need three volunteers."

A girl stepped forward, but Vron pointed to Greg, Dean, and Kyle.

"What's he up to?" asked Dean nervously.

"Do you think he knows it was us?" whispered Kyle as he moved in closer to Greg and Dean.

Vron did know. He had heard everything Greg said to Eliza as he lay on the ground.

Vron stared hard at the three boys. One by one they turned to stone.

There were gasps from the bleachers. Some of the students started to run away in fear. Others started laughing, thinking it was a Paxan joke.

74

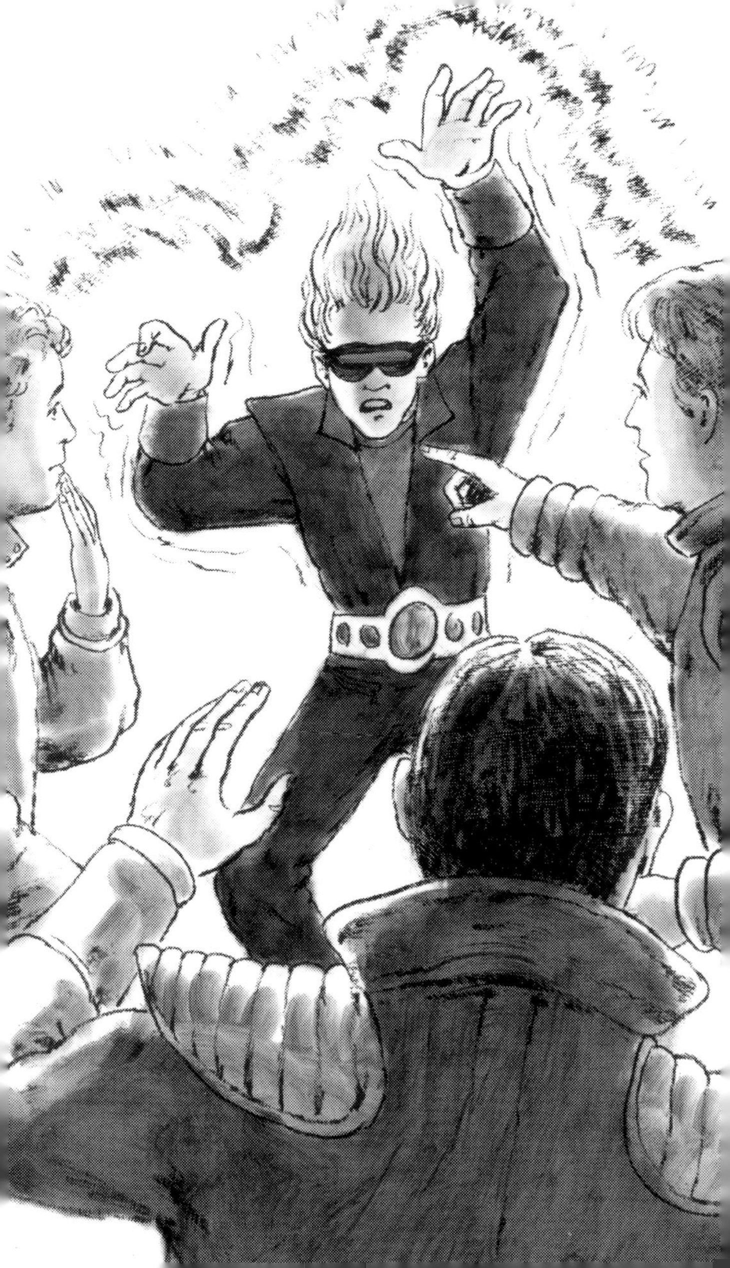

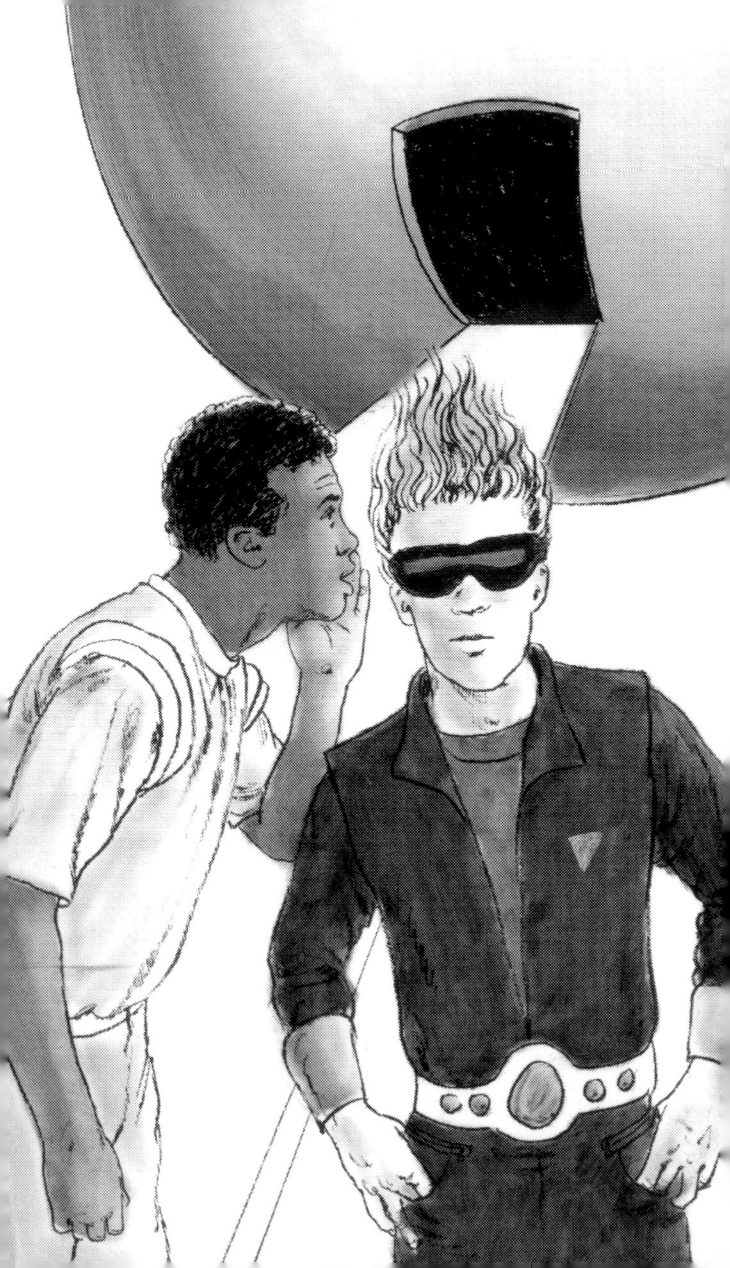

But Eliza knew the truth. Greg had pushed Vron too far. She stared in terror at Greg—or what had been Greg. Could he still be alive?

"Please, Vron," she cried. "Please turn them back!"

At that moment, the Paxan spaceship appeared in the sky. Soon it landed and Darryl walked down the ramp.

"What's going on?" Darryl asked. Then he saw the three stone boys. He ran over to Vron and spoke to him softly in the Paxan's own language.

Vron nodded. He turned back and nodded at Greg, Kyle, and Dean. One by one the statues returned to life.

Vron walked over to Greg and extended his hand. "I'm sorry," he said. "I should not have lost my temper."

Greg took Vron's hand. "I deserved it," Greg said. "I'm the one who should apologize. I was jealous of you. I got so mad, I was out of control."

"You didn't need to be jealous," said

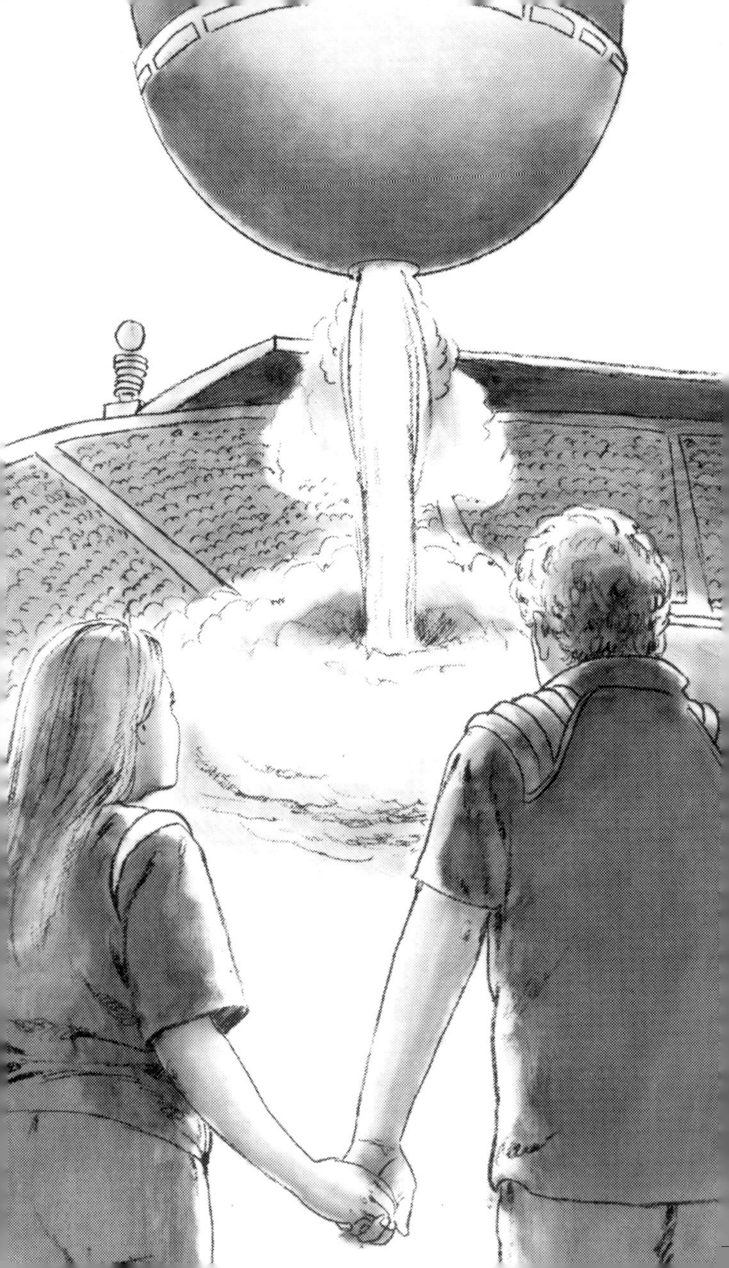

Vron. "I just wanted friends. It was clear to me that Eliza cared deeply for you. She still does."

They shook hands. Then Vron turned to Eliza. "And you have been a wonderful friend, Eliza. Thank you for teaching me so much about life on Earth."

Eliza gave Vron a warm, strong hug. Then Vron walked up the ramp to the spaceship to go home.

Eliza turned to Greg and hugged him, too. "Are you all right?"

"My head's killing me," he said.

"That'll wear off soon," said Darryl, patting his friend on the back. "Believe me, I know!"

"I'm sorry for what happened, Greg," Eliza said. "I should have included you more while Vron was here. I'm sorry, and I've missed you."

"I missed you, too," said Greg.

"Hey, what about me?" Darryl said. "Didn't anyone around here miss me?"

Greg and Eliza started laughing. "Yeah, big guy," said Greg. He slapped his friend playfully on the shoulder. "We missed you, too."

Just then Eliza heard a soft sound. It was like a thousand tiny wind chimes. She felt her pendant gently vibrating against her chest.

Greg reached out and took Eliza's hand in his. Eliza gave his hand a quick squeeze. Together they watched the spaceship rise up into the air, headed back to Pax.